The Not-so-Nice Victorians

W
FRANKLIN WATTS
LONDON • SYDNEY

This edition first published in 2005 by
Franklin Watts
338 Euston Road
London
NW1 3BH

Franklin Watts Australia
Level 17 / 207 Kent Street
Sydney
NSW 2000

Editors: Lesley Bilton, Paula Borton, Suzy Jenvey
Designers: Jason Anscomb, Kirstie Billingham
Cover illustration: Andy Hammond
Consultant: Dr Anne Millard, BA Hons, Dip Ed, PhD

A CIP catalogue record for this book
is available from the British Library.

ISBN 0 7496 6316 2

Dewey Classification 823.914

Printed in Great Britain

The Not-so-Nice Victorians

Contents

Chimney Charlie

by Roy Apps

Illustrations by Julie Anderson

1

A Hard Day's Work

Charlie Thompsett shivered. The room was cold, for no fire had been lit in the hearth that morning.

"Take yer coat off, boy!" commanded Scroat. "And yer boots!"

Jeremiah Scroat was a Master Sweep.

Charlie was his climbing boy and this was his first job.

Scroat began fixing a cloth across the hearth. "Should be easy enough this one, even for a new 'un like yourself," he said, curling his lip in a leer. "About 35 feet tall and 15 by 10 inches wide, I reckon."

Charlie shivered again. Not just from cold, but from fear.

"Get behind the cloth," Scroat hissed. "Come on, boy! We ain't got all day. There's another six chimneys to do before the morning's out!"

Charlie stepped behind the cloth. It was pitch black. Through the material he could make out Scroat's shadow. As the cloth moved he saw it fluttering like a black, evil ghost. Suddenly the ghost was gone and Scroat was standing at his side.

"Up!" he snarled.

Charlie pushed his brush up the chimney. Too late, he remembered that he was supposed to pull his sweep's cap down over his face. His brush dislodged a pocket of soot which dropped straight into his eyes, making them sting. But before he had time to wipe them, Charlie felt a pair of rough hands grab his ankles and lift him right off the ground.

"Go on! Like I showed yer! Push with your elbows and knees. Push!"

Numb now with fear, Charlie pulled his sweep's cap over his face and forced himself up. Holding his brush above his head with one hand, he pushed against the sides of the chimney with his body.

Slowly Charlie inched his way up the inside of the tall chimney like a human caterpillar. As he swept the soot fell over him on its way down to the hearth below. It was so dark he found it hard to tell if his eyes were open or shut. It was silent too, except for the tap-tap of his brush as it searched out the path of the chimney above him.

Eventually Charlie felt a sudden blast of cold about his ears. He was near the top. With one final push his head

cleared the chimney stack and he found himself peering out across the frosty, early morning roof tops of the town.

"What are you doing up there, boy?" A voice echoed faintly but harshly up the chimney below him.

Charlie pressed his knees in and began to slide back down the chimney. He pushed himself down the small bend faster than he should have done. The rough chimney bricks ripped at his shirt and trousers and then at his elbows and knees. He landed in a sooty heap at Scroat's feet, his elbows and knees bloody and stinging with pain.

While the housekeeper paid Scroat, Charlie put on his jacket. He looked around for his boots and with alarm saw Scroat giving them to the housekeeper – for money! Scroat caught his look.

"You'll not be needing these, boy," he said to Charlie. "You can walk barefoot. It'll save you having to take 'em off and put 'em back on each time we get a job." He laughed coarsely.

Outside most of the rest of the world was still not awake. Scroat set off. Charlie, barefoot now and laden with his bag of soot, trotted after him.

"Sw–e–e–p!" called Scroat as they walked along. "Sw–e–e–p!"

Sometimes a maid or housekeeper would call them in, and then up another chimney Charlie would climb. By the time they had finished he could hardly bear to touch his knees and elbows, let alone press them against the rough chimney bricks.

Charlie followed Scroat towards his lodging. The sack of soot on his back weighed heavy from half a dozen chimneys. The smells drifting from the various hot pie stalls teased Charlie's nostrils. He was hungry.

"Jes' you wait here for me, boy," growled Scroat.

Charlie was pleased to see his master stepping into a butcher's shop. When he came out Scroat had a small packet tucked inside his coat.

Scroat's lodging was a tiny basement room in a tall house a few streets up from the river. Even on a cold night like this, the smell of raw sewage and dead fish wafting up from the river was disgusting. In summer, Charlie guessed, it would be even worse.

Scroat lit a small candle and a very small fire. Then he took from his jacket the package he had bought in the butcher's. Charlie's eyes looked up expectantly.

"What do you think I've bought then, boy? Pork chops or some tripe, perhaps?" he sneered, unwrapping a bottle from the paper. Easing off the cork he poured some of its contents onto a filthy rag. Charlie watched, fascinated.

Suddenly Scroat grabbed Charlie and started rubbing the rag on his elbows and knees.

"Yee–argh!" screeched Charlie. "That hurts." It was the first thing he had said all day.

"Stop yer racket, boy!" yelled Scroat. "It's only brine. The salt water they keep

fresh meat in. Yer knees and elbows need hardening up and rubbing this stuff in for a couple of weeks will do the trick."

Come early evening Scroat gave Charlie half a bowl of broth and bread.

"That's all you're getting. I know better than to feed up a climbing boy. The more boys eat, the bigger they get, and thin boys are best for climbing chimneys."

Still covered with soot from his day's work, Charlie curled himself up into a ball in the corner. Scroat threw a sack over him, then set off in the direction of the nearest public house.

Charlie's whole body ached. He heard a scurrying sound, and then felt a plop on the top of his sack. Opening his eyes he found himself staring into the watery pink eyes of a rat. It looked as hungry as Charlie himself.

He sat up painfully and the rat scampered away through a hole in the floor. "Oh, to be a rat," thought Charlie. And, at that moment, he just knew that somehow he had to escape from the clutches of Jeremiah Scroat.

Slowly, bit by bit, he retraced in his mind the events that had led him to the dreadful circumstances in which he found himself ...

2

A Sudden Shock

The day before had started off pretty much like any other. Charlie and his mates, the Bromley brothers, were up to no good. They were on their way to visit a street of rich people's houses to play their favourite game – "Knock down Ginger".

This was, of course, Charlie's idea.

Proudly Charlie showed George and Billy Bromley a large bundle of string.

"Where d'yer get that?" George Bromley had asked.

"Friend of my Pa's," Charlie had replied.

Charlie's father had been a sailor and he had taught Charlie all kind of knots and hitches. His ship, *The Lady Gresham*, had been lost at sea the winter before last. As Charlie's mother had died shortly afterwards, he was being brought up by his elderly aunt.

Making sure nobody was around, Charlie skipped up the steps to the large front door and looped the end of the string round the door knocker. Then he tossed it over the brass lamp above the door and threaded it through the railings at the side of the steps. He carried on threading the string through the railings until he reached the end of the street. There he pulled the string. The knocker rattled with a satisfying thud-thud on the door. A maid came out with her face like thunder. Charlie, George and Billy couldn't contain their mirth. They all rolled round in one big, rollicking heap.

"Hey you there!"

Suddenly the boys saw the owner of the house, who had come out of the *back* door to catch them! They raced like the wind towards George and Billy's house.

"Charlie!" Liza, George and Billy's big sister, was at their front door. Normally she was a cheerful girl, but today her face was anxious.

"Charlie, you'd best get yourself home."

"Why?" Charlie felt a stab of panic in his stomach.

"Summat's happened." Liza grabbed him by the arms and gave

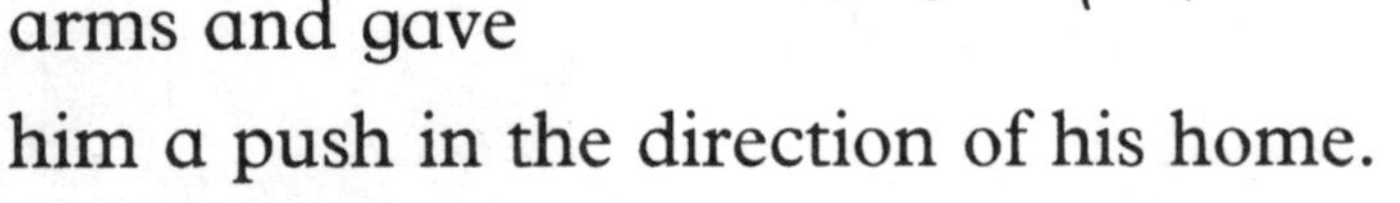

him a push in the direction of his home.

Charlie raced blindly along the streets until he reached his own house. Mrs Bromley, George and Billy's mother, stood in the hall.

"Oh Charlie Thompsett, what in the world's going to become of you?" she sobbed. "Your aunt, she's gone." Mrs Bromley shook her head sadly.

"Gone? Gone where?" Charlie's heart beat wildly.

"Heaven. I'm sure of that. She was an angel and a saint all rolled into one when she was living." She turned to Charlie. "Oh my poor lamb, whatever's going to become of you, now that all your relatives are dead?"

The undertaker came out of the house. "There's only one thing that can be done with him. He must be handed over to the workhouse!"

As soon as Charlie heard the word 'workhouse', he turned on his heels and

ran. No one was putting Charlie Thompsett into the workhouse!

He ran until he was exhausted. Then he walked until the night began to close in. He realised he had no bed, no money, and no food. Food could of course be stolen, but the penalties for theft were severe – prison, transportation, or worse. Charlie found an alleyway, pulled his thin jacket about him, and curled up on the cobbles. He was cold and uncomfortable, but more than that, he was tired. He drifted off into a deep sleep.

"Bet you'd fancy a slice of bread and dripping, eh boy?"

Charlie opened his eyes. He found himself looking up into a grimy, leathery face. The face broke into a terrifying grin, revealing a row of one yellow tooth and two black ones. Charlie was speechless.

"Orphan?"

Charlie nodded.

"This is your lucky day, boy!"

It didn't feel to Charlie like a lucky day at all.

"You've got a choice, boy," the leathery-faced man continued. "You can throw yourself on the mercy of the parish workhouse, or you can get yourself regular food, shelter and wages, by learning a trade."

"What trade?" asked Charlie quickly.

"One of the most honourable trades in the country," replied the man. "The trade of Chimney Sweep. My name's Jeremiah Scroat. Chimney sweeping's my trade and I need a boy apprentice. What do you say?"

There was only one thing Charlie could say.

"Yes, sir. That is if you'll have me please, sir."

Charlie spent the night at Jeremiah Scroat's lodgings. He was given a slice of

bread and dripping for supper, and another slice for breakfast the next morning. Then he and Scroat set off for the Magistrate's house to get the papers signed which would make Charlie a legal apprentice. On the way back Scroat bought Charlie a sweep's cap with a brass badge. Scroat's name and address were engraved on the badge.

"Do you read, boy?" asked Scroat later as they sat in his lodgings.

"A little," said Charlie.

Scroat waved Charlie's apprenticeship papers – called indentures – in front of his face.

"It says here that you're bound to me as apprentice now for seven years."

Charlie nodded.

"It means that I own yer," growled Scroat. He put his face close to Charlie's. "I own yer," he repeated with an ugly sneer, "just as I might own a dog."

3

Escape from Scroat

Now, one day into his career as an apprentice sweep, Charlie lay shivering and aching under his sack. He must have drifted off to sleep, for the next thing he knew he was being shaken awake roughly by the arm.

"Get up, yer lazy bag o' bones!" roared Scroat. Soon Charlie was scrambling up the first chimney of the day. He could hardly bear the pressure on his grazed elbows and knees, but he pushed on. He had decided on a plan of escape.

As his sooty head popped out of the top of the chimney, he looked around him. The grey slates glistened with frost. Instead of inching himself back down the chimney, Charlie carried on pushing up. In no time at all he was on the roof. His knees hurt, but he didn't care. He was free. He started crawling faster, when suddenly a slate slipped and crashed to the ground. Charlie froze, but it was too late. The noise had alerted the household – and Scroat! Charlie climbed painfully down the drainpipe, not to freedom, but to a thrashing.

"Yer won't try that again in a hurry, will yer, my lad?" snarled Scroat.

"No, sir."

"Because you'd only get taken to the workhouse," said Scroat, smiling evilly at Charlie. "And yer better off with me, ain't yer?"

Slowly the days passed and winter turned to spring. The pain in Charlie's elbows and knees wore off, but not his fear of the tall, dark, narrow chimneys. That fear was getting worse. One morning he found himself so scared he just sat, wedged in the bottom of the chimney, unable to move.

"I'll get you up that chimney, yer lazy good-for-nothing," growled Scroat.

Charlie suddenly smelt smoke. He

heard the crackling of burning wood, and then he felt a stab of pain as flames licked the soles of his feet. Scroat had lit a fire! He was "smoking" him up! Charlie let out a scream of horror. He forgot his fear of chimneys in his terror at being burned alive. Up the chimney he went, choking in the smoke, his feet toasted like tea cakes.

On their way home from work that day Scroat stopped at a public house. Charlie

sat on the steps outside, hoping that his master would bring him something to eat.

Afternoon was darkening into evening when a rough hand yanked Charlie inside the pub. The air was thick with the smell of beer, tobacco and sweat. A gang of sailors were dancing, arms interlocked, singing lustily and out of tune. In the far corner sat Scroat, slumped over a table, drunk. Opposite him sat a younger sweep with a little pile of money in front of him. The man looked up at Charlie.

"So you're Scroat's apprentice?"

Charlie nodded.

"Not any more you ain't. He's just bet all his possessions on a game of cards with me, and he's lost. You're mine now. Come on!"

Scroat suddenly woke up from his drunken stupor. "You may have won the

boy – and a lazy, bone-idle boy he is – but you ain't won his clothes. I made no mention of what he was wearing. His clothes belong to me!"

Charlie backed off in horror as Scroat lunged at him, trying to rip his jacket off. Suddenly the younger man raised his fist and slammed it into Scroat's chin. In a flash Scroat was lying senseless on the floor. A cheer went up from the sailors as Charlie was pulled through the swaying crowd by his new master. "Come on, lad. I've got cold beef and pickles at home."

While they tucked into supper, Scroat's vanquisher introduced himself. "I'm 'Arry 'Awkins, sweep. That's 'Awkins with an

Haitch. No need to look at me like I'm going to eat you. I've always fancied having an apprentice. I was a climbing boy myself once, see."

* * * *

It was strange, but Charlie was never frightened of chimneys when he was with Harry. Unlike Scroat, Harry didn't walk the streets looking for work, he had regular customers who booked him.

Then, a few months later, came the most terrifying day of Charlie's life. It began when they were standing outside a fine, large house.

"This is our first job today," said Harry. "Mr Parslow's new place. Ain't it grand? I used to do his old house, but this is my first time here."

"Mary will bring you a mug of tea," Mr Parslow said as Charlie began to take of his jacket. "It's hard and thirsty work you boys have to do."

Charlie liked what he saw of Mr Parslow, but he didn't like what he saw of his chimney. He poked his head round the screen.

"It ain't 'arf narrow," he said to Harry.

"Let's go up onto the roof," said Harry, "and we'll

see what it looks like from up there."

An icy wind was blowing across the rooftops.

"This looks wider," said Harry. "You'll be fine if you buff it."

"I ain't buffing it!" protested Charlie. "I ain't going stark naked down no chimney for no one." So Charlie took off his shirt, but kept his trousers on.

Down the chimney he went. As he edged down, he felt the sides of the chimney tightening on him. Then he

reached a kink in the flue and found that he couldn't push himself round the corner.

"Harry?" Charlie's voice was small with terror and foreboding. "Harry, I'm stuck!"

Scroat had been right – big boys don't make good climbing boys. And since he had been working with Harry, Charlie had been

eating better and growing bigger by the day.

"Push yourself back up!" shouted Harry.

Charlie pushed, but found he hadn't got the room to ease himself back up either. Panicking, he tried wriggling some more. The more he struggled, the more he stuck fast. Through his head flashed the tales he had heard of climbing boys suffocating to death in narrow chimneys. He opened his mouth to scream, but found his mouth was already filling with soot.

Harry's shouting had been loud enough to be

heard throughout the house. Suddenly, Mr Parslow burst in.

"What's going on?"

"Boy's stuck," said Harry worriedly.

Mrs Parslow appeared and began to sob. "He won't die, Horace, will he? Not in our chimney?"

But Mr Parslow was already heading for the door. "I'll fetch a builder! We'll take the chimney down brick by brick if we have to!"

Charlie found himself drifting between

wakefulness and sleep. He did not know how long he had been in the chimney when he heard the thump, thump of hammer and chisel on brick.

They lifted him out wheezing and

spluttering and laid him on the floor in the Parslows' bedroom. After he'd coughed up a stomachful of soot they gave him a cup of beef tea to sip slowly. Mr and Mrs Parslow wept with relief. Harry hugged

him. "I thought you were a gonner that time," he said. There were tears of joy in his eyes.

They swept no more chimneys that day.

"You've got too big for the climbing lark," said Harry. "And I'll tell you another thing. After what happened today, I don't feel like sending any more lads up

chimneys. The trouble is, what are you and I going to do for a living? Sweeping's the only trade I know."

It was a dismal supper for the two of them that evening. Cold mutton and gherkins had never seemed so dry before.

Suddenly, Harry and Charlie were startled out of their misery by a knock at the door.

"Mr Hawkins? My good sir, I'm glad I've found you!"

There on the doorstep stood Mr Parslow.

4

A New Partnership

Mr Parslow declined Harry's offer of a gherkin and a glass of ale.

"I'll come straight to the point," he said. "Mrs Parslow and I were absolutely terrified by what happened when you swept our chimneys this morning."

"We were a mite anxious ourselves there for a bit, weren't we Charlie?" answered Harry.

"Yes," said Charlie, breaking out into a sweat just at the thought of it.

"So this afternoon, Mrs Parslow and I called on a friend of ours, a Mr Amos Catchpole. He is very active in the local branch of the Society for Superseding the Employment of Climbing Boys. Indeed, he is the inventor of Catchpole's Chimney

Cleansing Machine."

Harry raised a suspicious eyebrow.

"Mrs Parslow and I have joined their number. In short, we don't believe you should be sending boys up chimneys any more."

"Oh you don't, don't you?" Charlie noticed that Harry was getting rather red in the face.

"No," Mr Parslow continued. "And to that end, I am prepared to buy you one of Mr Catchpole's chimney cleansing machines."

Charlie's eyes lit up with excitement. He had heard talk of chimney sweeping machines, but had never seen one. It was Harry who spoke, though.

"I'm much obliged, I'm sure," he said, "but I don't take charity from any one."

"But Harry – " protested Charlie.

"And I'll thank you to let me speak in my own house," replied Harry, sharply.

"Of course, if you wish, you could treat my offer as a loan and repay me the cost of the machine at such time as you are able," added Mr Parslow quickly.

Harry cocked his head this way and that. "Hmm … perhaps, yes … I would be pleased to accept your kind offer."

Next day, Harry and Charlie set off from Mr Parslow's with the new chimney cleansing machine. It consisted of a large round brush into which were screwed a series of flexible rods. Through the rods ran a long piece of string, so that if any of the rods broke off in the chimney, they wouldn't get lost.

Charlie pulled at the string. "Just like 'Knock down Ginger'," he laughed.

Harry looked thoughtful. "The way I see it is like this – these here rods are heavy. I ain't going to be able to manage them and carry a bag of soot. And another thing. If while I'm setting up the screen, I've got a mate screwing the rods together, and if while I'm unscrewing them, that mate bags up the soot, I'll get twice as much work done and twice as

much work means twice as much money!"

With a start Charlie saw Harry disappear into a printer's shop. Charlie followed him.

"I want a new trade card," Harry was saying to the printer. "It's for 'Awkins, with an Haitch ..." He turned and winked at Charlie. " – And Thompsett, Chimney Sweeps."

A broad beam spread across Charlie's face. "You and me? Partners?"

Harry grinned. "It's the least I can do," he said. "If you hadn't got stuck up Mr Parslow's chimney, he'd never have thought of buying us a machine, would he now? Come on. Don't stand there gawping. We'll go and buy a nice bit of tripe and onions for our supper. And some potatoes. You'll need feeding up if you're going to help me carry those great rods!"

CLIMBING BOYS and GIRLS in Victorian Times

During the late eighteenth and early nineteenth century, coal became a popular household fuel. Coal requires a good draught, and so fireplaces and chimneys were made narrower. These narrower chimneys became blocked with soot. It was thought that the only thorough way of cleaning these chimneys was to send children up them with a brush. The first chimney sweeping machine was invented as early as 1803, but most people still preferred to use children.

Pauper children

Many sweeps' boys were "parish children", orphans who had been taken to the parish workhouse. The "parish" – the town or village council – could avoid having to pay for food and keep for these orphans if they sold them to chimney sweeps.

Apprentices

Sweeps' boys were apprentices. The local magistrate signed "indentures", legal documents meant to ensure that apprentices were properly trained and looked after by their masters. In practice, these "indentures" were often worthless.

Injury and death

Being a climbing boy or girl was a dangerous occupation. Many children were killed after being suffocated or burnt in chimneys. Others fell off slippery roofs. Endless hours spent in dark and narrow chimneys meant that climbing boys and girls often didn't grow properly. They might have damaged backs and knees. The rubbing of elbows and knees against the rough brickwork also gave them bad sores, and the soot damaged their eyesight.

The climbing boy who survived

Despite terrible conditions some climbing boys and girls did survive. Peter Hall became a climbing boy at the age of six and a half, but he managed to live through all the hardships he experienced. When he grew up he travelled round the country checking up on master sweeps who were cruel to their apprentices. He took many of them to court, achieving no less than 400 convictions against them for breaking the law.

The size of chimneys

If you want to imagine what it was like climbing a tall narrow chimney, cut out a piece of paper 23 centimetres square. That is the size of many of the chimneys children climbed. Then cut out a piece of paper 18 centimetres square. It is on record that a six-year-old girl climbed a chimney as narrow as this.

Convict!

by

Julia Jarman

Illustrations by Liz Minichiello

1

Wrongly Accused

Mary Catchpole hobby-horsed with the broom as she swept the cottage floor, and her sister Susan laughed.

"Get on with it, Mary, or mother will wallop you!"

"She'll have to catch me first!"

Mary was "jumping" the fender when their mother came in with a basket.

"Stop fooling, girl, and take the men their lunch. Run, now! They've been ploughing since dawn!"

Mary tugged at the latch on the door leading to the back yard, and started along the cart track towards the fields.

Twenty minutes later she was sitting on the plough-horse's broad back in the sunlight, watching her father and brothers eating their hunks of bread and cheese.

Mary loved horses. She loved it when the breeze lifted their manes and fluttered their feathery fetlocks.

She loved the jingle of the harness and the smell of sweat and leather.

This was her favourite part of the day.

It was on her way back that things started to go wrong. Mary was leaning across the gate to Hall Field gazing at the squire's new chestnut hunter, when she heard a scream.

"Help! Come quickly!" A maid was running out of the old wheelwright's cottage.

When Mary reached the kitchen, Mrs Denton lay stretched out on the cold stone flags of the kitchen floor. She looked very ill

"Doc..." she gasped.

The doctor - of course!

The maid was dithering, so Mary took charge. Ordering her to fetch water from the pump for her mistress, Mary set off at a run

Unfortunately, the doctor's was five

miles away. Even if she ran every step it would take an hour.

But then she had what seemed like a good idea.

Seconds later she was on the chestnut mare's back.

She must get to the doctor.

She must get to the doctor.

That was the only thought in her head.

She must get to the doctor.

She must get to the doctor.

Her thought kept time with the horse's hoofs as she raced through the countryside.

Going up Bishop's Hill she slowed a bit.

Then there was the town below her, with its twelve church towers and the river curving around it, but she didn't notice much of that.

The doctor - that was her only thought.

She kicked the horse faster.

However, it was market day. She had to weave her way around hay wagons, pig carts and carrier vans to reach Orwell Place where the doctor lived.

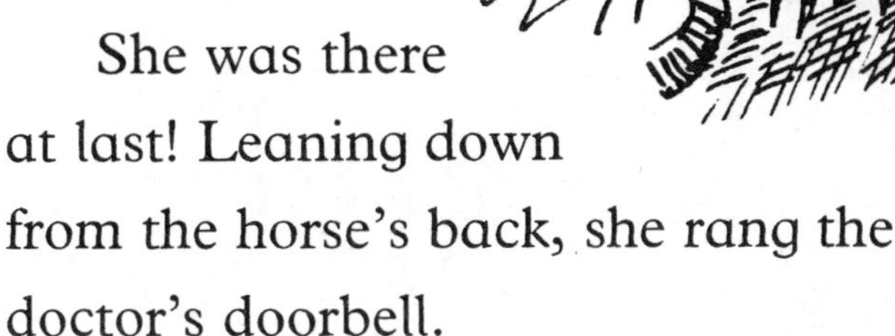

She was there at last! Leaning down from the horse's back, she rang the doctor's doorbell.

Doctor Stebbings praised Mary for acting so quickly. Then he harnessed up his cart and clattered off down the lane in a cloud of dust.

Mary patted the horse and felt relieved. But then her troubles really began.

A crowd of people had gathered in the doorway of the alehouse at the bottom of the lane, attracted by all the hoofbeats and shouting.

Mr Pryde, the squire's head man, pushed his way to the front of the crowd. He looked angry.

"Mary Catchpole! What are you doing with the squire's new hunter? Stealing's a transporting offence, you know!"

"I didn't steal it!" cried Mary.

"Tell that to the judge!" he said, stooping to examine the mare's leg.

"You've ruined this horse, galloping over the cobbles. There's a damaged tendon here."

He sent someone to fetch the constable.

The crowd were muttering and staring at Mary, who began to worry. People were saying the horse had cost a hundred guineas. Others were muttering that it might have to be shot.

The constable arrived and put chains round Mary's wrists. She tried to hold her head high as he walked her to the gaol.

She was not guilty.

She had *borrowed* the horse.

HMP

The constable handed her over to the gaolkeeper as silent faces stared at her from barred windows.

"Welcome to 'appy 'all," said a not-so-silent one.

"Silence, Nell!" shouted the gaoler. He opened the door of an empty cell.

Things went quickly from bad to worse. First, Mary was charged with *wilfully stealing and damaging a horse worth one hundred guineas.*

Then they said she would have to stay in gaol for fifty-seven nights - and days, of course - until her trial at the next Quarter Sessions.

Prison was dark and cold, but she was fortunate in a way. At least the gaol was clean.

And after a time, Mary was given some work to do sewing the blue calico uniforms they wore in the gaol.

But she was very lonely. That was part of the system - *Separate and Silent*, they called it.

Mrs Ripshaw, the gaoler's wife, told her she should use the time on her own to think

about what she'd done and repent. If she showed she was sorry at her trial, the judge might give her a lenient sentence.

"How long would a lenient sentence be?"

"Three years in gaol, or transportation for five years."

Mary didn't dare ask what a severe sentence would be.

To be locked up for three years! To be shipped to Australia for five!

Mary's mother came to visit on the night before the trial. She looked as if she'd been crying.

"We've got to move away, Mary. Your father's lost his job on account of what you did. The squire turned us out of the cottage this morning."

Mary felt dreadfully sorry and angry at the unfairness of it all.

"Promise me something, girl," said her mother. "Plead guilty at your trial. They say it helps your sentence if you show you're repentant."

"No," said Mary stubbornly.

She didn't feel sorry. She'd done a *good* thing. She had only *borrowed* the horse.

"I'd rather tell the truth, mother. Send word when you're settled. I'll be joining you there soon."

On the morning of the trial, Mary was taken from her cell when it was still dark and hand-cuffed to two other prisoners.

They travelled in the back of an open cart, and as it got light people could see them as they passed through the villages. Mary thought she would die of the shame.

The journey took five hours. It was late morning by the time the cart drew up around the back of the court building. The prisoners were taken down some steps and into a room like a cage.

Mary's case was the first to be called. Her hopes rose when Doctor Stebbings spoke up for her. She could hear the murmurs of approval all around the courtroom as the Doctor explained how her actions had probably saved Mrs Denton's life.

But they fell when Mr Pryde and then the squire himself took the stand.

There'd been a lot of horse stealing lately, the squire said. The lower classes were becoming too free with his property. They needed to be taught their place.

Mr Pryde said he had often seen Mary hanging around the horses' fields.

He'd even caught her in the stable yard once, patting the hunters. He said Mary had stolen the horse deliberately for a free ride, and she was using Mrs Denton's illness as an excuse.

Other witnesses were called - all tenants or servants of the squire - and they said the same thing.

Mary described exactly what had happened and said she was sorry she had lamed the horse.

Several more people spoke up in Mary's favour. They said she was honest, and worked hard.

The judge took a long time to make up his mind. Mary was beginning to feel quite hopeful.

But then he pronounced her guilty.

He said Mary had shown unbecoming pride in her actions. He said he was making an example of her, so that others would learn not to do the same thing.

Sentencing her to seven years' transportation, he ordered her to be taken to Portsmouth where a convict ship was waiting to sail.

2

Just a Number

"Number 78 - keep moving!"

The overseer's voice broke through the icy fog on the freezing dockside.

As she dragged her chained feet towards the convict ship, Mary remembered thinking that nothing could be worse than gaol.

But in gaol she'd had a name.

Now she was just a number.

It was on the papers that said she was a convict. It was on the arm of the grey uniform she wore. It was on the leg irons which had already made her ankles raw.

"Pull yer drawers down a bit and tuck 'em in!" Nell, number 77, called over her shoulder.

Nell, who had called out to Mary the day she'd arrived in gaol, was full of handy hints.

Mary had got to know her on the four-day journey to Portsmouth, and had learned that she'd stolen a handkerchief - to get money to feed her little brothers and sisters, she said.

"My mistress 'ad dozens of handkerchiefs. I didn't think she'd miss one. 'Ow many noses 'as she got, after all?" Nell had laughed.

Mary still didn't know what to think. Stealing was wrong, but Nell didn't seem one bit ashamed of herself. Very few of the other convicts did, either. Certainly not

Lizzie, Number 76, who had got caught stealing spoons - to get food for her family, she said. Her dad and brothers hadn't been able to earn enough money, now that farmers were paying their labourers so little.

Nell and Lizzie were talkative, but most of the convicts were as silent as Mary as they shuffled towards the *Sirius*, or stepped warily on to it.

It didn't look very safe.

But they were even more dismayed when they saw the barracoon in the hold of the ship where they were going to spend the next eight months.

How would they all fit in?

"By being packed like blooming sardines," Nell said.

"Or flipping jars of jam," said Lizzie.

Mary simply wished she could die there and then. Dark and airless, the prison stank already.

What would it be like when all hundred convicts were inside, packed three to a bunk?

What would it be like when it got hot?

When the buckets - four between all of them - were full of waste?

"Just think, our Clem paid for this!" said Nell.

She'd already told them about her older brother who had bought a ticket to Australia, to start his own farm there as a free settler. There was plenty of land in Australia, people said. Not like at home.

Nothing would stop Nell looking on the bright side. She was sure she was going to meet up with Clem eventually, even though she hadn't heard from him since he'd gone three years ago. She'd asked her family to get word to him that she was on her way.

But as Mary lay between Nell and Lizzie - the sea only inches away from her ear - she couldn't think of anything to look forward to.

Didn't convicts have to work like slaves for the free settlers? Or for the government?

Men in chain-gangs building roads, women in factory prisons sewing army uniforms?

If they got there. The ship looked old and it creaked a lot, shuddering when a bigger than average wave hit the sides.

What would it be like when they were at sea?

3

A Terrible Voyage

She was soon to find out.

Suddenly the roof of the barracoon shook as feet above moved quickly.

And there were shouts - about anchors being raised and main sails hoisted.

The fog had cleared, quite suddenly.

They didn't see, because you couldn't see anything from the barracoon. But as icy winds started to whistle through gaps in the woodwork, and the *Sirius* started to rock, they knew that the tide was coming in.

Shortly after that things on the ship felt different.

"We're on our way," said Nell.

Someone else said, "Good riddance to Great Britannia!"

But everyone else was silent - all thinking of the families they were leaving behind no doubt.

Mary tried not to think of hers - her mum and dad and sister Susan, her brothers Charles and Ned and the baby, little Tom - but she couldn't help it.

Would she ever see them again?

She thought of her friends, and of Doctor Stebbings and Mrs Denton who had both spoken up for her in court.

In the small bag of possessions tied round her waist, she had letters from them describing her good character. They would help her get a good position when she was free, they said.

Doctor Stebbings had said she mustn't lose hope. Lots of convicts eventually made good lives for themselves in Australia.

Mary tried to be optimistic. It helped a bit when the captain appeared in the doorway of the barracoon and said he was instructing the second mate to

remove their leg irons.

"On the strict understanding that you co-operate fully in the orderly running of the ship," he said. "Any bad behaviour will result in leg irons being restored and remaining for the rest of the voyage."

"Good old Cap'n Isaiah," said Nell, when at last they could stretch their legs.

But Lizzie said, "It's not because he's good, stupid. It's because he'll be in trouble if we're all lame when we get there and can't work. And we're not likely to try and escape are we?" They hadn't seen land for days.

"Why do you call him Isaiah, anyway?" she added. "Isn't his name Williams?"

"'Cos one of 'is eyes is *'igher* than the other, of course! Look at 'im next time," said Nell.

Lizzie laughed and so did Mary.

Nothing got Nell down - not their diet of ship's biscuit and water.

Nor the hours spent in the stinking barracoon - they were allowed only one hour on deck a day.

Nor the terrible seasickness which Mary

and nearly everyone else got as they crossed the Bay of Biscay.

As the ship reared from side to side, and the waves thundered and roared and water spurted through the scuttles, Nell did what she could to look after people. And she tried to keep the barracoon clear of vomit by sluicing it down with sea-water.

Her good humour kept them all going, and - when she stopped being sick - Mary really did start to feel hopeful too. Maybe things would turn out right.

They did see some amazing things - dolphins and whales and porpoises, and brilliant-coloured birds.

And one day Mary found Nell standing on her hands.

"What are you doing?" she gasped, because you could see Nell's drawers!

Fortunately all the sailors seemed to be asleep.

"Practising walking upside down," said Nell.

"Why?"

"We're going to the other side of the world, aren't we? So we'll have to."

Mary laughed, but it made her think. What would Australia be like? Some people called it the end of the world - but Nell, wonderful Nell, made it sound like an adventure.

So it was terrible when she became ill.

4

No Water

It couldn't have happened at a worse time.

For days the ship hadn't moved. It was blistering hot and there was no wind.

The sun blazed directly overhead and their water ration had been cut to half a pint a day. Nobody felt well - or looked well.

So Mary who had a terrible headache and blistered lips didn't notice that Nell was any worse than the others, till Nell suddenly flopped forwards. They were on deck at the time.

Then, of course, she sprang into action.

Lizzie helped Nell into the shade below.

Then Mary went to Captain Williams to ask for water.

It was obvious that Nell needed some desperately.

But to her amazement, he said no, not until the evening. Water had to be strictly rationed, he said, to make the supply - already low - last as long as possible. If they ran out they would all perish.

But he did agree to come and look at Number 77.

Mary led him to where Nell was lying, now thrashing her arms around.

"Clem...hankie...water..." She was obviously delirious.

The captain asked if she had a rash. It was hard to say. Her skin was so red anyway. So was everyone's.

He asked if she had vomited.

Lizzie said she had.

He said, "She'd better go into isolation. She may be infectious."

A few others had been taken ill, he said, and he'd got the crew to clear a space in the stores, near the bow, where they could be kept separate from the rest of the ship in case they passed on the disease.

There was quite a lot of space in the stores, after four months at sea. He ordered a sailor to take them there.

Lizzie helped Mary carry Nell.

The sailor kept his distance, they noticed.

He told them to put Nell inside the door and leave.

"Leave?" Mary counted six other convicts, including an old woman, all lying on the straw pallets.

The sailor said, "Come on."

Mary said, "But who's looking after them?"

He looked at her as if she was stupid.

"They can't look after themselves," said Mary.

Now it was obvious that the captain's only concern was to keep the ill convicts away from the rest.

The sailor said, "I've orders to take you back to the barracoon."

Mary refused to go. So did Lizzie.

Nell must be looked after. Her skin was burning hot and dry. If they couldn't give her a drink, they must cool her body somehow.

The sailor went off - that was something.

As quickly as they could, they took off Nell's prison dress. Then Mary stayed with Nell, fanning her, while Lizzie went to hang the dress over the side.

Their plan was to wrap Nell in the wet dress to bring her temperature down.

They knew better than to give her - or themselves - sea-water to drink.

But when Lizzie came back - with Nell's dripping dress - Captain Williams was with her.

18

"The punishment for disobedience is a return to leg irons," he said.

Mary said, "Put me in leg irons if you must, but let me stay."

He said he couldn't risk her life.

She said she'd risked her life already.

If Nell had got an infectious disease, she had probably got it too by now.

He said, "If you stay now, you stay in isolation with her for the rest of the voyage."

Mary agreed to that. So did Lizzie, but the captain said he wouldn't let two of them do it. His task was to deliver a full contingent of convicts fit for work.

But Lizzie was allowed to leave supplies outside the door each day. She brought their water ration that evening.

For the rest of the night and all through the

following day, Mary tended to Nell and the others as best she could.

But by the next nightfall the old woman had died.

When Lizzie brought their rations she said there was no water. However, a cloud had been sighted. The crew were spreading sails over the deck to collect every last drop of water if it did rain.

Mary told Lizzie about the old woman. Soon after she'd gone, a sailor appeared with a large canvas bag.

He told Mary to put the old woman's body in it and leave the bag outside the door. He said there were more bags if anyone else died.

Later that day, Mary heard hymn singing.

In the evening Lizzie described the funeral.

The old woman's body, covered by a union jack, had been slid down a plank into the sea, she said.

She asked how Nell was.

Mary said she was dreadfully still and quiet.

They were both silent then, thinking the same thing, till Mary said, "Nell's not going to die. I won't let her."

But all she could do was keep Nell as cool as she could, by sponging her body with sea-water.

Then in the middle of the night, she heard a new sound - of rain on canvas! - though she didn't realize it was that immediately.

Suddenly the ship was rocking violently.

Thunder rolled and cracked.

Round them a storm was raging.

Even so Lizzie managed to get fresh water to Mary and the invalids.

"Drink lots, Mary," Lizzie said. "I know you've been sharing your ration with Nell."

I'll bring more as soon as I can."

She did too - and more after that. For three days the storm raged, filling the water barrels and speeding the ship south. And slowly, day by day, Nell began to get better.

Five months later they caught a glimpse of land. Strange, purple-coloured hills and tall bright red geranium plants, as big as trees. Gradually the coastline curved to form a wide sandy bay.

Botany Bay.

5

A New Life

As the *Sirius* sailed towards the docking platform, Mary steeled herself for another test.

She saw people waiting. Government officials and free settlers looking for labour, the captain explained.

Long before you could see their faces, Nell scrutinized them.

"Poor Nell," said Lizzie. "She really thinks her Clem will be here to welcome her."

It was humiliating, shuffling on shore in leg irons.

It was even worse being inspected like cattle, as they moved towards an enclosure on the dockside.

"Number 27! Number 33!"

Some numbers were called out as people fancied the look of particular individuals.

Mary clutched her letters from Doctor Stebbings and Mrs Denton, but she noticed that people were mostly interested in what the convicts looked like.

Then she was brought to a sudden halt by Nell, who'd stopped walking.

"What's the matter?" Mary thought she'd fallen ill again.

Nell didn't answer. She was staring across at a brown-faced curly-haired man, standing on his own to one side of the crowd.

“Keep moving, 77!”

“Nell, move!”
Mary urged.

Then another
voice rang out,
“Number 77!
I’ll have
Number 77!”

As the
curly-haired man stepped forward, a
government official noted his request.

Mary’s heart sank - so they were going
to be split up. Her greatest dread.

They reached the enclosure.

Now consultations took place between
officials and “purchasers”.

A factory owner wanted thirty convicts.
He took the first thirty in the line.

The head of the orphanage wanted
three for domestic service.

She chose numbers 34, 39 and 45.

Then the curly-haired man claimed Nell, who had tears in her eyes. She was murmuring, "Clem, Clem. Is it really you?"

He muttered, "Quiet, Nell. If they know we're related, they might not let me have you."

She whispered, "Take Mary and Lizzie too. 78 and 76."

He said, "I need farm-hands. Men really."

She said, "They saved my life, Clem."

He said, "I'll have Numbers 78 and 76 too."

It was a bit of amazing good fortune. Word had reached Clem that Nell was on her way, but he'd come that day expecting a consignment of male convicts. He needed labourers for the farm he had started.

So Mary, who had always preferred

76
78

horsework to housework, started her new life in Australia on Clem Palmer's farm and soon became an excellent ploughwoman. She grew to like her new life in Australia.

When she had worked her sentence she decided to stay there, and eventually she became Clem Palmer's wife.

But she never forgot her family. She named her favourite farm horse Susan, after her younger sister.

CRIME and PUNISHMENT in Victorian Times

This book is based on the true story of Margaret Catchpole, who really was found guilty of horse-stealing and transported to Australia, where she served a seven-year sentence.

Victorian Punishments

In early Victorian times, crime was on the increase and the law dealt out harsh punishments to convicts - convicted prisoners. Until 1841 all murderers and some thieves received capital punishment - the death penalty - and were hanged. After 1841 only murderers were executed.

Thieves were sometimes punished by being flogged. Watched by the public, the constable would administer a number of lashes.

Prison

Many thieves - even if they stole something small, like a handkerchief - were punished by being sent to prison. Children were treated exactly the same as adults.

Some old prisons - like Newgate in London - were filthy and overcrowded. Men, women and children prisoners were all mixed together. In the new "model" prisons, like Pentonville and Ipswich, the Separate and Silent system was practised. Prisoners were kept in solitary confinement to think about their crimes and repent.

Transportation

This form of punishment - also called deportation - began in 1787 and continued through Victorian

times (1837-1901). It was seen as a good way of ridding the country of criminals, and of developing Australia as Britain's new colony using the criminals as cheap labour. Over 108,715 convicts had been transported by the time the system was abolished in 1868!

Life in Australia

Convicts had to work for no pay. Their treatment varied. Some, especially convicts who stole or got drunk, were flogged, kept in chains, and given the worst jobs. Others found to their surprise that they were better fed than they had been in England.

Most convicts stayed on in Australia after their sentence had ended, partly because they couldn't afford the fare back, and partly because they saw Australia as a country full of good opportunities.

Bodies For Sale

by
Mary Hooper
Illustrations by Greg Gormley

R.I.P.

1

In the Hospital

"Fresh sawdust!" came the call from the hospital operating theatre.

Jack Bean, waiting in the hallway outside the theatre, pulled himself together. He didn't much like going inside because he was never quite sure what he might see.

Dr Patterson was an expert with the saw, very speedy at cutting off legs and arms. Although Jack was used to seeing a lot of blood about the place, he was a bit squeamish about anything else. Once he'd gone in and tripped over a whole leg that had been left on the floor!

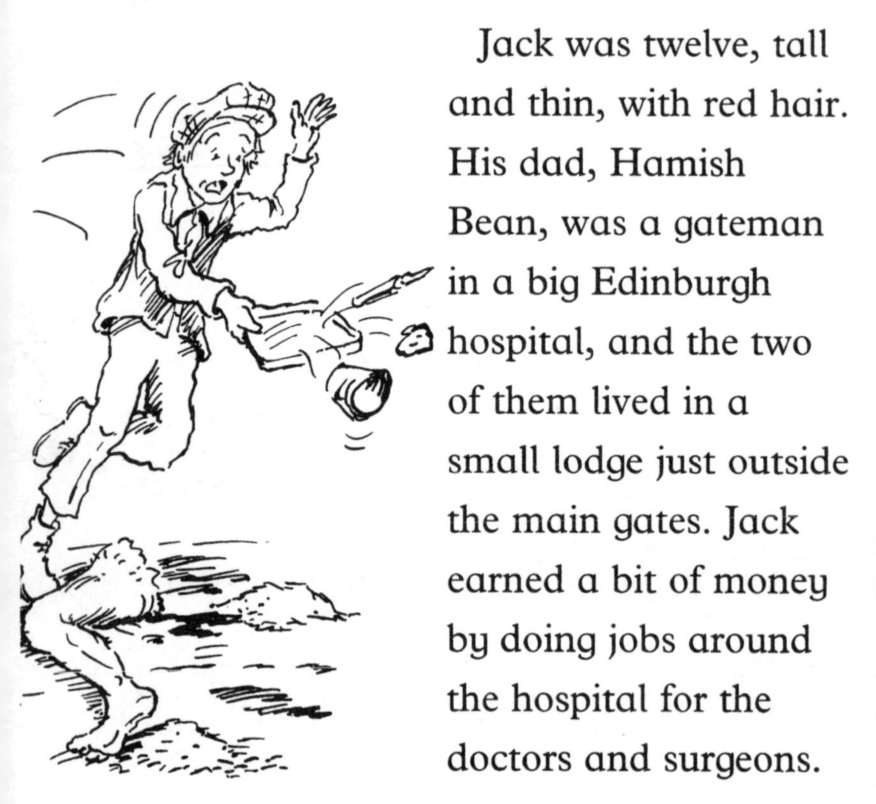

Jack was twelve, tall and thin, with red hair. His dad, Hamish Bean, was a gateman in a big Edinburgh hospital, and the two of them lived in a small lodge just outside the main gates. Jack earned a bit of money by doing jobs around the hospital for the doctors and surgeons.

"Sawdust!" came the roar again. This was needed, Jack knew, to help mop up the blood. He took a deep breath, picked up a box of fresh sawdust and carried it in.

It was crowded in the operating theatre. Dr Patterson was a brilliant surgeon. Whenever he was working, a crowd of other surgeons and doctors, students and important hospital visitors gathered to see him in action.

It was as if they were there to see a fight or watch a play, Jack thought, for the high, domed room was ringed round with places for people to stand and watch the

operations. There were about sixty people there, talking amongst themselves, shouting questions and jostling for the best views.

Dr Patterson was wearing a filthy jacket stained with blood. He seemed to have a cold, for he sneezed twice right over the man lying on the wooden bed in front of him.

Jack glanced at the face of the poor patient, who had his eyes tightly closed and was muttering to himself. Jack knew that before he'd come into the theatre, he would have been given a few glasses of beer to dull the pain of what was to come.

Jack put down the box of sawdust on the floor and waited to see if Dr Patterson wanted anything else. He glanced about him – there were no spare arms or legs around.

"Move yourself, laddie!" someone shouted. "You're blocking my view!"

Jack jumped and scuttled out of the room, glad to get away – and hoping he'd never, ever need an operation.

Dashing down the stairs, he had the bad luck to bump into the stooped figure of Angus Crabtree – an evil individual who'd recently come to work at the hospital. Old Angus was an odd-job man and, so rumour had it, was willing to do anything, no questions asked. After a day's work he could still be found hanging about outside the hospital, coaxing a penny or two out of the sick people who had come for help.

"Out of my way!" Angus snarled, aiming a blow at Jack's backside with his stick. "And I'd better not see you on my patch again, either."

"What do you mean?" Jack asked, pressing himself against the wall to get as far away as he could from the man.

He knew what Old Angus meant, though. One of Jack's best money-earning jobs was collecting leeches – the blood-sucking, worm-like creatures that were used by the doctors to get blood out of a patient. Jack had discovered a stretch of marshland by the river where a good clutch of leeches could often be found.

"I've seen you and your mangy cur hanging round the marshes," Old Angus said. "That land is mine by right. The leeches are mine."

"They're not yours," Jack said bravely. "I was finding leeches there before you arrived. You must have followed me in order to find that spot!"

Angus grabbed him by the collar. He had a patch over one eye, but the other was glittering dangerously. "So what if I did? You be civil to your elders and betters. If I see you there again it'll be the worse for you. D'you hear me?"

Difficult not to, Jack thought, for Angus's ugly face was only inches from his own.

"I hear you," he said. But if you think I'm going to give up my leech-gathering, he thought, then you've got another think coming.

2

In the Graveyard

"I think I might go out later tonight," Jack said to his dad a week or so later.

Hamish Bean looked up from mending a pair of boots. "Oh, you do, do you?"

"Well, I can't find the time to get my leeches during the day – I'm so busy at the

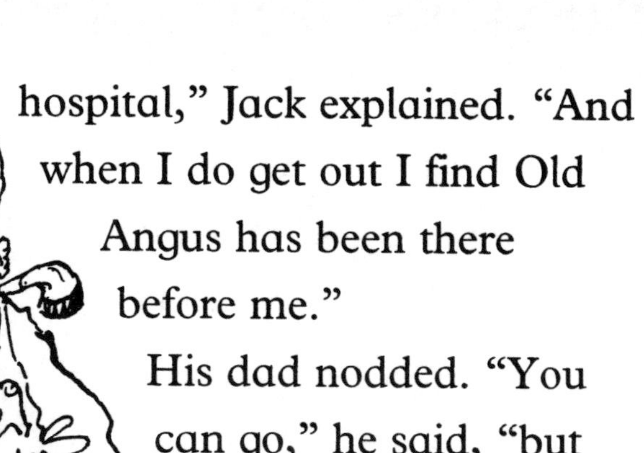

hospital," Jack explained. "And when I do get out I find Old Angus has been there before me."

His dad nodded. "You can go," he said, "but wrap up warm and carry a lantern. And take Braveheart for company."

Jack bent down to pat the scruffy terrier who lived with them.

"'Course I will," he said. "He's only a wee dog," Hamish Bean went on, "but he can bark loudly in the dark and scare people off."

At about ten o'clock, Jack, after promising to stay away from ale houses and other trouble spots, tied an old sack around his shoulders to keep warm, and set off.

"Stay close by, Braveheart," he said to the dog as they walked down the dark streets. It was windy and the scudding clouds only revealed the moon now and again. "Be ready to bark at anyone who wants to make trouble." The little dog wagged his tail cheerfully.

But there was precious little trouble on the Edinburgh streets that night. Jack made his way to the marshes, hung his lantern on the overhanging branch of a tree, and soon managed to get a whole jar of wriggling black leeches.

He held them up to admire them.

"Well worth missing an hour or two's sleep," he said to Braveheart. "I wish I'd brought two jars."

The dog, who was huddled on the riverbank out of reach of the leeches, gave a whine. Nights should be spent on a warm pile of straw with a juicy bone between his paws, not on a cold and windy riverbank, thank you very much.

"All right," Jack said, checking to make sure that none of the leeches were actually sticking to his skin and sucking his blood. "We can go back home now."

The two of them set off, walking back by the route they'd taken earlier. "I'll sell the leeches to the doctors tomorrow, Braveheart," Jack said, "and see you get a good marrow bone as payment for coming along with me."

Apart from the chimes of a distant clock striking midnight, the city was almost silent as Jack trudged home.

It was then that, quite suddenly, he heard the roll of wooden wheels and the dull thud of a horse's hooves as a horse and cart turned into the street.

Jack quickly put out the candle in his lantern. He didn't think it was anything to worry about – probably just a market-stall holder or trader on his way back from a trip out of town – but he wasn't going to take any chances. He pressed himself against the wall until the cart passed.

"Keep quiet, Braveheart!" he said, pushing the dog to sit down. "We haven't got anything worth stealing, but they may not know that."

The cart passed them, the horse plodding slowly up the hill. A little way further on, it came to a halt.

"Now, why has it stopped?" Jack whispered. "What's there to stop for?" He tried to peer through the darkness but he couldn't see without his lantern. It wasn't until he had crept almost up to the cart that he realised it was outside the church at the crossroads.

Jack peered over the wall. The church had a small graveyard attached to it and the moon had just come out, reflecting on the tombstones, so that they shone with a dull, spooky light.

He saw two figures standing by a grave, whispering. One had just been digging – he was holding a spade and Jack could see a pile of freshly dug earth at his feet.

"They don't usually dig graves at this time of night," Jack whispered to Braveheart. "There's something strange going on."

Jack focused on the figure with the spade – a tall, thin man wearing a patch over one eye and a battered top hat. He bit back a gasp of horror and astonishment. Old Angus! But what on earth was he doing?

As Jack watched, the other man jumped into the newly dug hole and threw out a large cloth followed by a limp figure which he heaved up to Old Angus waiting above. The two men then hoisted it up and began to walk with their grisly burden through the graveyard.

Jack put his hand on Braveheart's shaking body, and shrank back against a tombstone. He could scarcely believe what he was seeing.

"Easy pickings!" Old Angus gloated to his companion as they passed by. His coat brushed the side of the stone behind which Jack and Braveheart were quaking.

"Aye!" said the other man. "Reckon we'll do another this week. You get me word where and when."

Jack crouched, rooted to the ground, until the two men had loaded their bundle on to the cart and moved off down the road. Then he jumped up and ran for home, as if there were a hundred devils after him.

3

A Horrible Tale

"Dad, Dad!" Jack cried, shaking his father. "Wake up!"

"Wha . . . what's happened? Is there a fire?" Hamish Bean sat up in bed, rubbing his eyes.

Jack held his lantern aloft. "No, not

that. I've seen something very strange," said Jack with a shiver. "Something really horrible!"

His dad closed his eyes again. "Get your leeches, did you?"

"Yes, but – oh no!" Jack said, remembering he'd left the jar on the ground in the churchyard. "It's nothing to do with them. Braveheart and I saw Old Angus and another man digging up a grave. We watched them pull out something and . . . and I'm sure it was a body! Then they threw it on a cart and took it away. But what would they want a dead body for?"

Hamish nodded. "Och," he said and sighed. "I wondered if that was his game."

"What game?" Jack asked. "What do you mean?"

Hamish groaned and turned over. "I'll tell you in the morning. Now let your poor old father get his rightful sleep."

Jack shook his dad again and tried to pull him into a sitting position. “No! Tell me now. I’ll never get to sleep unless you tell me!”

There was a long pause before Hamish spoke. “Well, then,” he said slowly, “you’ve heard tell of Dr Knox at the hospital, haven’t you?”

Jack nodded. He knew that Dr Knox was an anatomist, a highly skilled doctor who’d found out many things about the workings of the human body.

"Well, Knox and Old Angus are thick as thieves," Hamish said.

Jack nodded, puzzled. "Yes?"

"And there's rumours that Old Angus does secret work for Knox. No questions asked."

"What sort of secret work?"

Hamish Bean tapped the side of his nose. "You can guess, can't you? Dark deeds, laddie!"

Jack shook his head, bewildered. "What sort of dark deeds?" he asked. What his dad was hinting at was just too gruesome to be true.

There was another long pause. "Well," said Hamish, "you know Dr Knox does demonstrations to explain the workings of the body to young gentlemen doctors?"

Jack nodded.

"Well, there's never enough corpses for him to practise on. Never enough bodies for him to show people things like where the heart is, where the lungs are, and how a body's put together with its bones and muscles. Only a few convicts' bodies a year are given to the hospital, and that's not enough for his dissections."

Jack's mouth dropped open. "You mean Dr Knox uses . . ."

"He uses other bodies," his dad said. "Dead bodies that arrive in the night out of nowhere. Bodies that have been stolen!

Stolen from graveyards, dug up from their rightful resting place in the dark ground and prised unlawfully from out of their coffins."

Jack gasped. "And Old Angus gets the bodies for him?"

His dad nodded. "We've thought for some time that he might be at that game. There've been many mysterious comings and goings – and lately the old devil has been boasting in the tavern about the pile of money he's got put away. On an odd-job man's wages!"

"But that's horrible," Jack burst out. "Can't anyone stop people robbing graves?"

His dad shrugged. "There's some that try, but it's not easy for a man to protect his dead kin from tomb-robbers."

Jack shivered as his dad sank down into the bed again and yawned loudly.

"Angus has been dressed a deal smarter lately, too. Two suits when an honest man has only one threadbare jacket to his name."

"What do you mean? He's buying himself more clothes?"

Hamish Bean grunted and settled down to sleep. "Angus buying them? That'll be the day. No, I mean he's wearing dead men's clothing. Corpse's clothes."

Jack shuddered. "*Corpse's clothes*," he murmured to himself. "That man's evil."

4

The Plot Thickens

"Not so fast there, young Jack. I want a word with you. Have you got any leeches to sell?"

Donald Buchan, one of the trainee doctors, stopped Jack as he ran down the hospital corridor early the next day.

Jack, who was on his way to deliver some fairly clean bandages from the washroom in the basement to one of the wards, shook his head. "Sorry," he said regretfully. "I'm fresh out of leeches."

"That's a pity," Donald said. "I need a new stock. There's a shortage you know. I had to use the last lot twice over."

Jack looked puzzled. "How did you do that?"

"I squeezed 'em out!" said Donald cheerfully. "I squeezed all the blood out of them and stuck 'em on again!" He pulled a large watch out of his pocket. "Got to go. Dr Knox is carving them up at eleven o'clock!"

"In the theatre? What's he carving?" Jack asked eagerly.

Donald smiled at Jack's interest. "He's doing a dissection on a body to show where the muscles are and the lines they follow." He felt Jack's upper arm. "These are some of your muscles, up here!" he grinned. "Want to come to the theatre with me and see?"

"No, thanks," Jack said. He hesitated, then asked innocently, "When they do this stuff, this *dissection* stuff, where do they get the bodies from?"

Donald shrugged. "Search me. Knox always seems to have a regular supply, though. The more dissections he can do, the more money he can get from the chaps who want to learn from him."

He glanced at his watch again "And now you'd best be delivering those bandages, young Jack!"

Thoughtfully, Jack continued his way back to the ward.

❖

It was seven o'clock in the evening and Jack and Braveheart were following Old Angus, at a safe distance, through the streets of Edinburgh. Old Angus had a rolled-up bundle under his arm and evidently didn't want to be seen. He was walking in the shadows, very close to the wall, his head well down.

Reaching a corner, he looked carefully all round him and then entered a shop – a vast shop which had its window crammed with all sorts of things: vases, boots, jewellery, lamps, hats and small pieces of furniture. From the three golden balls hanging over the entrance, Jack knew that it was a pawnbroker's shop. More than once he'd been sent by his dad to such a place to borrow money, leaving Hamish's watch as security.

Jack peered through the dusty window as Old Angus approached the counter and rolled out his bundle. It seemed to contain a man's shirt, two pairs of boots and a dark tweed jacket. There was also something else, something small, which might have been a gold ring.

Jack's heart began to beat fast as he pressed nearer to the window. He hadn't looked closely in the graveyard the night before, but he thought he recognised the shirt as the one worn by the dead man.

And Old Angus was probably pawning the dead man's wedding ring, too.

Some money changed hands, and Old Angus came out, hat well down on his head. Jack followed him down the road and into a busy market place.

Old Angus went up to the man working on the pie stall and Jack, under cover of the crowd, went nearer and saw him pass the man a bag of coins.

"Tonight," Jack heard him say. "Midnight. St Agnes."

And then he slipped away into the night.

Jack's heart started to beat very fast. There would be more body-snatching that night. And he knew where.

5

Braveheart to the Rescue

"You'd better not be playing a joke on me, my lad," said McTavish, the local sheriff. "I don't like being got up from my warm bed in the middle of the night."

"No, honestly!" Jack said, running swiftly with Braveheart beside the sheriff.

"I heard them arranging to meet here at midnight."

But what if they weren't there, Jack thought. What if he'd misheard Old Angus and got the church wrong, or the two men had changed the time?

It was Friday night, so Jack's dad was still at the tavern spending his hard-earned wages. Jack hadn't been able to tell him what was happening, or ask him to come along to the sheriff's office with him. He just hoped he'd done the right thing.

Jack's worst fears were realised, though, when they reached the churchyard. Everything was very quiet, and in the moonlight the place looked a picture of peace and calm.

"So where're your grave-robbers?" McTavish asked. "All's well here so far as I can see."

"Look near the new graves!" Jack said, pointing to the far side of the churchyard.

McTavish scowled. "Nothing but a wild-goose chase," he muttered to himself, but he followed Jack, holding his lantern aloft.

"Here!" Jack called him over to a wall. "Look what's here!"

Jack was standing beside a new grave.

The fresh flowers and rough wooden cross which had marked the grave had been thrown to one side, and a large pile of newly-dug earth lay beside the deep hole.

"Look!" Jack pointed down the hole. "The coffin's there and the lid's open!" He stepped back a little, too frightened to look any further.

McTavish strode over and looked

down the hole. "There's no body in that coffin," he said after a moment. He patted Jack on the shoulder. "Looks like you were right, laddie. There's been some wicked doings tonight, no question of it. The resurrectionists have been here, plying their evil trade."

"But they've got away!" Jack said with disappointment. "They must have got here early. Old Angus has got away with it again!"

"They come by night and steal away by night," said McTavish. "And where they'll strike next is anybody's guess."

"We can only just have missed them!" Jack said, feeling upset and baffled.

Just then, there was a scuffling on the

street side of the churchyard, followed by a frantic barking.

"That's Braveheart," Jack said. "He's found something!"

Jack and McTavish ran across the cemetery, racing between the gravestones.

There in the street stood the horse and cart. Two men were attempting to load a long, lumpy shape. Dancing round their legs, nipping their ankles, was Braveheart.

"You two! Stay where you are!" McTavish's voice boomed out.

Old Angus cursed Braveheart, then aimed a kick at him and missed. In doing so he fell sideways against the cart. The bundle he was holding dropped to the ground and the dirty carpet around it fell open. Jack and McTavish gasped. There on the ground lay the body of an old man partly wrapped in a white sheet.

Jack gulped. Some poor old man. Someone's relative who hadn't been allowed to rest in peace, but who'd been dug up out of the ground.

"Halt!" McTavish called to the robbers. "You are disturbers of the dead and I arrest you in the name of the Law!"

Old Angus fell against the cart and his companion sank to the ground. "I told you we were taking too many," he muttered.

Jack hung back, not wanting to be seen. As the sheriff went forward with his handcuffs, Jack called softly to Braveheart to come away, and quietly they left the churchyard by the front gate.

Jack's step was light as he walked through the streets. McTavish had told him that there would be a large reward.

He could buy a new suit for his dad and plenty of bones for Braveheart. And not only that – he'd be able to gather all the leeches he wanted from now on. The marshland was his again.

Whistling to himself, Jack went home. His dad would be back from the tavern now, and he wanted to tell him all about his big adventure.

GRAVE-ROBBERS in Victorian Times

A good fresh corpse could be sold for £10 – a great deal of money in Jack's day, so grave-robbing was a popular crime. In an attempt to prevent the "resurrectionists" (thieves who stole bodies from graves) people started to build lodge houses at cemetery gates. Relatives would employ a man to sit up all night with a gun to watch over the dead. Rich people had their kinsmen buried in double-barred iron coffins to stop intruders forcing their way into them.

Dr Knox

Dr Robert Knox really existed. He was an anatomist – a very clever man who found out lots about the way our insides work. Students flocked to see him cut up bodies in his Edinburgh hospital. But there were never enough dead bodies to work on, and Dr Knox never asked questions about where they came from.

The Great Burke and Hare Scandal

Burke and Hare were two villains who brought bodies to the hospital for Dr Knox. They often didn't wait for the people to die naturally! In the Edinburgh area there were at least 16 murders committed by them between 1827 and 1829. Burke usually suffocated his victims and until quite recently it was said that people had been "burked" if they died in this way.

Anaesthetics

The poor patients in this book had nothing to put them to sleep, or to dull the pain of their operations. In 1846 a Dr Simpson first used ether as a painkiller, and in 1847 he discovered that chloroform was even better. In 1857 Queen Victoria used chloroform when she was having her ninth baby, and after that anaesthetics came into general use.

Hospital conditions

Hospitals in the 1840s were grim places. Only poor people went into hospital – and then just as a last resort. Many doctors, and most nurses, were completely unqualified – and, since no one regarded cleanliness as important, bandages and dressings were often used over and over again. Sheets on a bed were hardly ever changed, and baths and washing facilities were unheard of. Buckets on the ward were used as lavatories by patients and staff alike, and emptied once a day by someone like Jack. It was no wonder that those patients who could afford it always chose to be treated at home.

About the authors

ROY APPS

I was born in the middle of the last century, so it's no wonder I'm interested in anything to do with history. As well as *Chimney Charlie*, I have written about Saxon sailors, Viking warriors, Victorian pickpockets and Edwardian filmmakers.

JULIA JARMAN

I've written lots of books because I've been writing for a long time. Lots of them are historical. I love travelling back in time, but only to visit. There was so much unfairness and cruelty – as there is in *Convict!*. Luckily the true story on which *Convict!* is based had a happy ending – in Australia, a country I love. For more information visit me at www.juliajarman.com

MARY HOOPER

Historical books are my favourites. They did things differently then and you can have a lot of fun finding out exactly what everyone got up to. I did some of my research at The Old Operating Theatre in London which is very gory indeed! I found out about Victorian funerals and discovered that they were so worried about bodysnatchers that some families would employ a man to sit by a grave and guard it!

Acknowledgements

Franklin Watts would like to thank the following for the use of copyright material in this collection.

All books cited are originally published in the *Sparks* series by Franklin Watts.

CHIMNEY CHARLIE
Text © Roy Apps 1999
Illustrations © Franklin Watts 1999

CONVICT!
Text © Julia Jarman 1997
Illustrations © Franklin Watts 1997

BODIES FOR SALE
Text © Mary Hooper 1999
Illustrations © Greg Gormley 1999

If you enjoyed these hair-raising stories, why not read some bomb-blasted adventures about daily life in World War Two?

0 7496 6317 0